Beauty and the Beast

retold by Diane Stortz

Fairy Tale Classics

LANDOLL
Ashland, Ohio 44805

A long time ago, a rich merchant had three daughters. Two were proud, lazy, and thoughtless. But the youngest, named Beauty, was humble, hardworking, and kind.

The merchant lost all his money and had to move his family from a large country estate to a small cottage. The two oldest daughters fretted and complained and caused their father a great deal of grief. But Beauty took care of all of them and never complained. She was a comfort to her father.

One day, the merchant prepared for a journey to a distant town where he hoped to find work. "Bring us back some fine presents, Father," demanded the two oldest sisters.

"And what would you like, Beauty?" asked the merchant.

Beauty, remembering the lovely gardens at the country estate, said, "I only want your safe return, Father, and a red rose."

On his way to the distant town, the merchant rode into a swirling snowstorm. In the blowing snow he strayed off the path and lost his way. He had almost given up hope of seeing his family again when he smelled roses and felt warm air on his face. He had found an enchanted castle.

There was no one in sight, and no one answered the merchant when he called out, "Hello! Hello! Is anyone here?" The merchant took his horse into the stable, warmed and fed him. Then, tired and hungry, wet and cold, the merchant went inside the castle.

He found a warm, cozy room with a table laid for supper and a fire burning brightly in the fireplace. He ate, feeling all the while that he was being watched, and then he slept.

In the morning, the merchant saw that someone had put out a clean set of clothes for him. He ate and dressed and then went to the stable for his horse. Then he stopped in the gardens and picked a red rose to take home to Beauty.

Suddenly, an ugly Beast stood beside him. "Is this how you thank me for my kindness?" roared the Beast. "Have I not given you enough?"

The merchant cowered before the Beast. "Please," he said. "The rose is for my daughter, not for me. I meant no harm."

But the Beast was not moved by the merchant's pleas. "I will spare your life only if you bring your daughter here to live with me," he said.

In despair, the merchant returned home. The next day he brought Beauty to the castle. She was frightened by the Beast's face, but touched by the kindness in his voice.

"Will you live in the castle with me to spare your father's life?" asked the Beast.

"Oh yes, of course," said Beauty.

The Beast gave Beauty's father a chest of gold and told him never to return to the castle. Though it felt as if his heart were breaking, the merchant left Beauty to make the Beast's castle her home.

The Beast gave Beauty her own room, a closet full of lovely gowns, and a clock that woke her by calling her name. Every day Beauty explored the castle, and every night she ate dinner with the Beast. "He is frightful to look at", she thought. "But his manner is gentle and kind". Beauty found that she enjoyed being with the Beast and looked forward to seeing him.

After dinner, Beauty and the Beast strolled through the gardens and continued their quiet conversations. And always, the Beast would look at Beauty and say, "Tell me, Beauty... Am I very ugly?"

"Yes Beast, you are," was always Beauty's reply. "But I am fond of you just the same."

And then the Beast would ask, "Will you marry me, Beauty?"

But though she was fond of him, Beauty could not imagine marrying the Beast.

"No Beast, I can not," was always her reply.

One night in a dream, Beauty saw an ugly old woman. "Do not judge by appearances," the old woman said. "What is ugly on the outside may be beautiful on the inside."

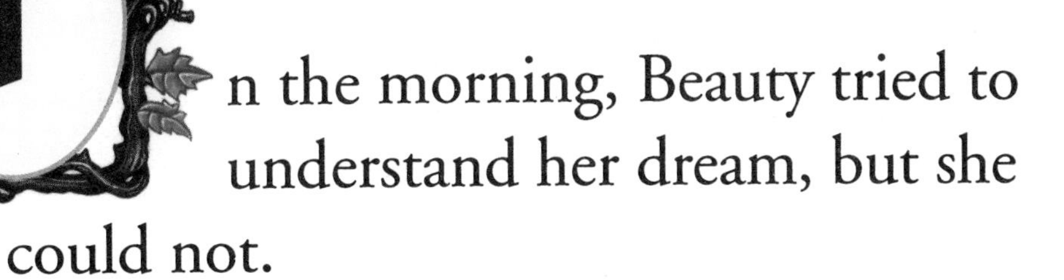

In the morning, Beauty tried to understand her dream, but she could not.

Soon after, the Beast gave Beauty a magic mirror. When she looked into the mirror, Beauty saw her father lying sick in bed. "Oh, Beast!" she cried. "My father needs me! Please let me go home to him."

"Promise to return to me," said the Beast.

"I will," said Beauty.

But she did not. She nursed her father back to health. His business had prospered, and her sisters had grown kinder.

Although she remembered the Beast fondly and sometimes wished to see him again, she could not bear to leave and break her father's heart again.

Then one night, Beauty looked into the magic mirror the Beast had given her. She gasped. In the mirror she saw the Beast, weak and about to die, under a tree in the castle gardens. Without a word to anyone, Beauty rushed to her horse and rode to the Beast's side.

He was so weak he could not move. Beauty lifted him into her arms and he opened his eyes to look at her one last time.

"Oh Beauty," he said. "Have you come back to me after all?"

"Yes, yes, dear Beast," said Beauty. "Please do not die. I never knew it until now, but I love you."

There was a sudden brilliant light, and then the Beast disappeared and in his place was a handsome prince.

"I was bewitched by a spell that could only be broken by someone who truly loved me in spite of my ugliness," explained the prince.

The prince and Beauty were soon married, and Beauty's father and sisters came to live at the castle, where they all lived happily ever after.